HUXLEY
AT THE CIRCUS

RODNEY PEPPÉ

FANTAIL

Huxley Pig woke with a yawn and a stretch and looked round his bedroom. At the foot of his bed lay the old suitcase his Granny had given him. It was packed full with the most wonderful dressing-up clothes.

"Squark!" called Huxley's friend, Sam Seagull, as he fluttered in through the open window.

" 'Morning, Sam!" said Huxley, rummaging in the suitcase. "What do you think I should wear today? How about this?"

He pulled a chef's hat out of the suitcase and tried it on.

"It's Huxley the Master Chef!" he announced. "Pork pies anyone? Oh, crumbs . . . what have I said?"

Huxley hurriedly stuffed the hat back into the case, but as he did so he spotted another hat – a strange red and blue one with a flower growing out of its hatband.

"Look at this hat, Sam," he said. "It must be part of a clown's outfit."

"It is a clown's outfit," he squealed, dragging the rest of the costume from the suitcase. There was a pair of spotted braces, a multi-coloured shirt, a pair of checked trousers, a red and white bow tie and an enormous pair of shoes.

"I'll look brilliant in this," said Huxley. "I'd make a fantastic clown, Sam. I can do all sorts of tricks and I'm great at making people laugh."

"Squark!" croaked Sam in disbelief. He'd heard some of Huxley's jokes and he wasn't so sure!

"I say! I say! I say!" cried Huxley. "What do you call a camel with three humps . . . ? Humphrey! Ha-ha!"

Sam groaned and covered his ears with his wings just in case Huxley should want to try out some more jokes on him. Huxley, however, was already thinking about something else.

"Where's that ball Granny gave me for my birthday?" he muttered, bending down to peer under the bed. "I'm sure I put it under here."

Huxley found the ball and rolled it out onto the floor. Then he quickly dressed himself in the clown's costume.

"I think a spot of balancing is called for now, Sam," he announced, stepping up onto the ball. With his arms outstretched to help him balance, Huxley wibbled to the left, wobbled to the right then crashed to the floor.

"Hmmm . . ." he pondered. "I might need a bit of practice there. I'm pretty good at standing on my head, though, Sam."

Sam could hardly bear to look as Huxley turned himself upside down to balance shakily on the floor, his legs swaying in the air.

"How's that?" puffed Huxley in an out-of-breath, upside down sort of voice.

"Squark!" Sam replied, rather impressed.

"I can do this for ages," Huxley gasped. Then he wibbled to the left, wobbled to the right and crashed to the floor again!

"Maybe juggling would be a bit less painful," he groaned.

"Now what can I use to juggle with?" Huxley wondered, scratching his chin. "I know! I put some hard boiled eggs in my lunch box yesterday. They're just the thing!"

Huxley opened his big red lunch box and found four eggs, one tucked away in each corner.

"Not bad, eh, Sam?" said Huxley, sending the eggs spinning into the air. Unfortunately, Huxley's chubby arms couldn't quite move quickly enough to <u>keep</u> the eggs in the air. They landed on the floor with a SPLAT! one after the other and a distinctly unboiled eggy mess oozed out around Huxley's feet.

"Oops!" said Huxley, shaking egg yolk off his foot. "I think maybe I forgot to boil them after all!"

Sam covered his beak with his wing to hide a little snigger but Huxley was already thinking about what to practise next.

"I'll try walking the tightrope!" he said.

"Squark!" gasped Sam. Generally speaking, pigs aren't all that good at walking on tightropes.

Huxley grabbed his dressing gown cord and tied it between two bedposts.

"I don't know why I didn't think of this before," he said.

With that he jumped onto the bed, stepped onto the tightrope – or rather, the tight dressing gown cord – and attempted to balance. With a wibble to the left and a wobble to the right, he toppled over onto the bed, bounced twice and landed in a heap on the floor.

"I don't think I'll bother trying that again, Sam," he said. "I'm really not too keen on heights."

Just then a gust of wind puffed in through the window. It lifted the bedcover off Huxley's bed and draped it over the dressing gown cord.

"Hey, look at that!" said Huxley. "The bedcover is just like a circus tent now – the Big Top!"

Exhausted after all his exertions, Huxley sat on the floor by his bed and drifted off into a colourful daydream about circuses, clowns and the Big Top . . .

"Ladies and gentlemen!" the Ringmaster's voice boomed out around the crowded Big Top, and a hush descended on the audience. "The Great Fettucini will now perform the most . . ."

"PSST!!" a whisper hissed from behind the backstage curtain.

"Not now," muttered the Ringmaster. "Can't you see I'm busy? The Great Fettucini, assisted by the not-so-great Horace will perform his death-defying tightrope . . ."

"PSSSST!!" came the whisper.

"Not now!" growled the Ringmaster. "The Great Fett . . ."

"PSSSSSSSSSSSST!!!" the whisperer would not give up.

"What is it?" rasped the Ringmaster, poking his head through the curtain.

"It's The Great Fettucini," said the not-so-great Horace. "Both his legs are in plaster after he fell through the safety net!"

"WHAT!?!" roared the Ringmaster. "I thought I told you to fix that net? Well, you'd better find someone else to walk the tightrope tonight or you'll be doing it yourself, understand?"

Horace understood, and the thought of walking the tightrope filled him with dread. It was then that he spotted Huxley.

"Huxley Pig!" cried Horace. "What are you doing here?"

"I was . . . er . . . hoping to join the circus," Huxley replied. Horace could hardly believe his luck.

"This pig," he muttered to himself, "might just save my bacon!"

"Do you need any clowns?" asked Huxley.

"Why, yes," said Horace, slyly. "Put your make-up on and get into the clowns' fire engine – our audience is waiting!"

Huxley was unbearably excited as he drove the ramshackle fire engine out into the circus ring to the applause of the crowd. Even so, he managed to steal a glance up towards the roof of the Big Top where he spotted the tightrope suspended between two platforms. "I'm glad I won't be going up there," he thought. "I'm definitely not too keen on heights like that!"

Pretending to rush to the scene of a fire, Huxley and Horace tripped over buckets, tangled themselves in hoses and soaked each other with water. In fact, they made the audience laugh so much that everyone's faces and sides were soon aching.

They chased each other around the ring with their huge clown boots pounding the sawdust and finally came to a halt at a mock doorway – Huxley on one side, Horace on the other.

"Knock! Knock!" said Horace.

"Who's there?" Huxley replied.

"Luke," said Horace.

"Luke who?" asked Huxley.

"Luke through the keyhole and see . . ." laughed Horace. Huxley, of course, stooped to look through the keyhole and a jet of water squirted straight into his face! Horace ran off, dropping his water-squirting flower as he went, and Huxley rushed after him.

Horace scrambled onto the fire engine and scuttled along the ladder with Huxley chasing close behind. At the end of the ladder, Horace dropped down into the driver's seat and pulled a lever. Slowly, the ladder began to rise, with Huxley clinging on as only a petrified pig can!

"Horace!" he screamed. "Get me down! I'm really not too keen on heights!"

Horace laughed wickedly at Huxley's predicament. The ladder continued to rise as he started up the fire engine and drove off. The rickety ladder shook and shuddered as the fire engine made its bumpy way across the circus ring. The audience applauded wildly, thinking this was all part of the show, but poor Huxley knew he couldn't hang on much longer!

Suddenly, the fire engine jerked to a halt, almost throwing Huxley off. Then, as the ladder swayed, he spotted a way of escaping.

"The tightrope platform!" thought Huxley. "That rotten rodent Horace has stopped just close enough for me to climb onto it. I'll have to be quick, though, before he moves off again!"

Huxley didn't really like the idea of standing on the tightrope platform, but it did seem safer than the fire engine's shaky old ladder, so he clambered across the short gap.

"Ha!" he yelled down to Horace. "That's put a stop to your little game!"

"That's what you think!" Horace yelled back, laughing louder than ever as he drove the fire engine out of the ring.

"What on earth can he mean?" wondered Huxley, but he didn't have to wonder for very long!

"Ladies and gentlemen!" announced the Ringmaster. "The Great Fettu ... er ... I mean, The Great Huxley Pig will now perform his death-defying tightrope walk – without the aid of a safety net!"

Huxley's heart sank. He'd been tricked!

A bright spotlight suddenly lit up the platform.

"B-but I'm really not too keen on heights," Huxley whimpered. The audience, however, was cheering far too loudly to hear him.

"Oh, crumbs!" thought Huxley. "They've all come here to watch someone walk the tightrope. It would be such a pity to disappoint everyone."

Huxley took a deep breath and placed one foot on the tightrope. Everyone fell silent as they gazed up at the bravest pig in the world. Holding out his arms for extra balance, Huxley moved off along the tightrope. He took one step, two steps, three . . . then he wibbled to the left . . . and wobbled to the right . . . the audience held its breath, but Huxley calmly recovered his balance and finished the act. The roar of applause that erupted was so loud that it made Huxley's big red nose buzz.

"Crumbs!" said Huxley. "It shows what you can do if you try, doesn't it?"

The next instant, Huxley found himself back in his bedroom again, sitting on the floor by his bed.

"Good gracious, what a vivid dream," he exlaimed. "The circus . . . the Big Top . . . the tightrope . . . I can almost still hear the applause from the audience."

"Squark!" said Sam Seagull, anxious not to be ignored. He had something to show Huxley.

"What's that you've found, Sam?" asked Huxley. "It's a circus programme and that's . . . but it can't be!"

Huxley stared in disbelief at the picture on the front of the programme. It was him – The Great Huxley, bravest pig in the world!

"Maybe it wasn't just a dream, after all," said Huxley. "The strangest things do happen when I wear something from Granny's old suitcase. Perhaps I should try some more juggling practice, just in case the circus ever needs me again. This time I'll boil the eggs first, though! Ha! Ha!"